The Peacock and the Crane

An Aesop's fable

Retold by Elsie Nelley
Illustrations by Tracie Grimwood

A long time ago,
there was a beautiful peacock.
He always walked around
waving his big tail.

Lots of birds and animals
told him he was very beautiful.

One day,
Peacock was walking along a path,
when he met Crane.

Peacock waved his tail.

Crane did not look at Peacock.
She was looking in the grass
for something to eat.

Crane walked on down to the pond.
Peacock walked down to the pond, too.

Peacock waved his tail up and down.
But Crane kept looking in the grass
for something to eat.

At last, Peacock said,
"Crane, please look at me.
I am very beautiful!"

Crane looked up.
"Are you talking to me?"
she asked.

Peacock walked in front of Crane.

"I am beautiful," he cried.
"Look at my feathers!
They are blue and green.
See how they shine
in the sunlight."

Crane looked at Peacock.
But she did not tell Peacock
that he was beautiful.

Peacock was very cross with Crane.
"You are a silly bird!" he said.
"You are not beautiful like me.
Your feathers are white,
and your legs are much too long!
Look at them."

Then, Peacock waved his tail again.
"Look at **my** feathers," he cried.
"**I** look like a beautiful rainbow!"

Crane looked down at herself.

Yes, her feathers were white.
She had long legs and long toes.
She had a long neck and a long beak, too.
And she had very long wings.

Crane looked at Peacock and she said,
"Peacock, **you** are the silly bird.
I can fly up to the clouds.
I fly to places that are far away from here.
Every day I look down
and see beautiful things."

Crane flapped her long wings and flew up into the sky.

Peacock watched Crane. “I have a beautiful tail, but I cannot fly like Crane,” he said to himself sadly.